CROCO'NILE

ROY GERRARD

Farrar, Straus & Giroux
New York

In ancient Egypt, long ago,
Beside the River Nile,
A brother and a sister
Found a baby crocodile.

They fed it lots of bread and dates,
And as it grew and grew,
It stayed the friend of Hamut
And his sister, Nekatu.

Each morning when the girl and boy
Came down to have a swim,
Their trusty croc was waiting
For the fun they'd have with him.

One day they climbed aboard a boat
Whose crew had gone to dine,
And mischievously hid there
In among the jars of wine.

The naughty twosome stayed concealed
Until the break of day.
By then their little village
Was a hundred miles away.
Although the crew weren't really cross,
They wondered what to do—
Returning was too risky,
For the floods were overdue,
And as the Nile would soon become
A mass of waves and foam,
The stowaways must quickly
Find a temporary home.

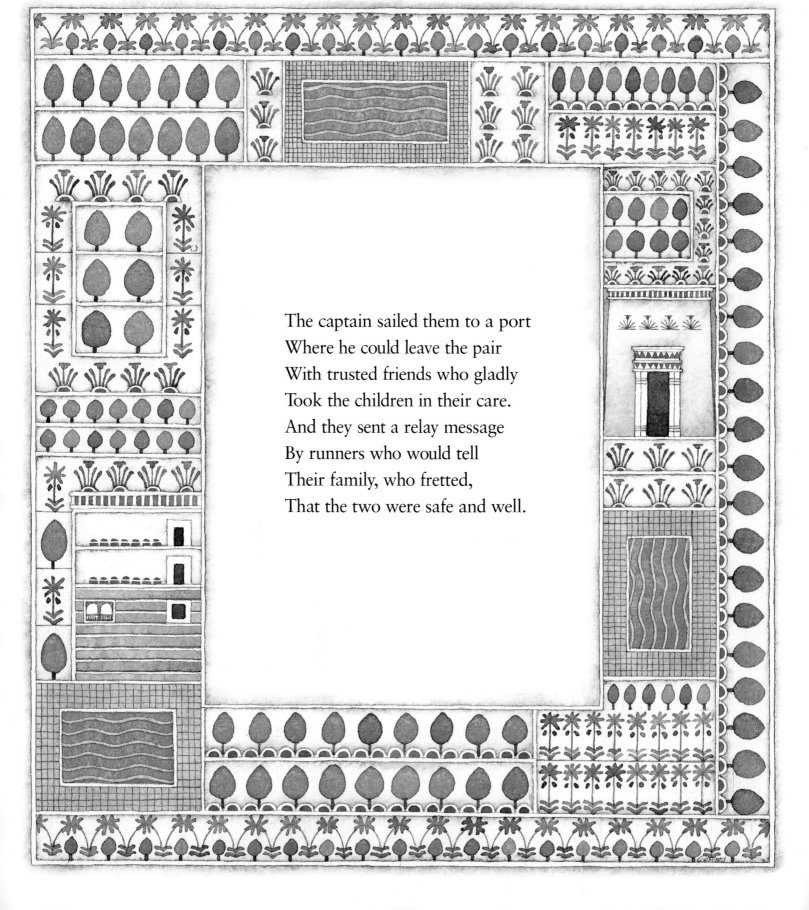

The captain sailed them to a port
Where he could leave the pair
With trusted friends who gladly
Took the children in their care.
And they sent a relay message
By runners who would tell
Their family, who fretted,
That the two were safe and well.

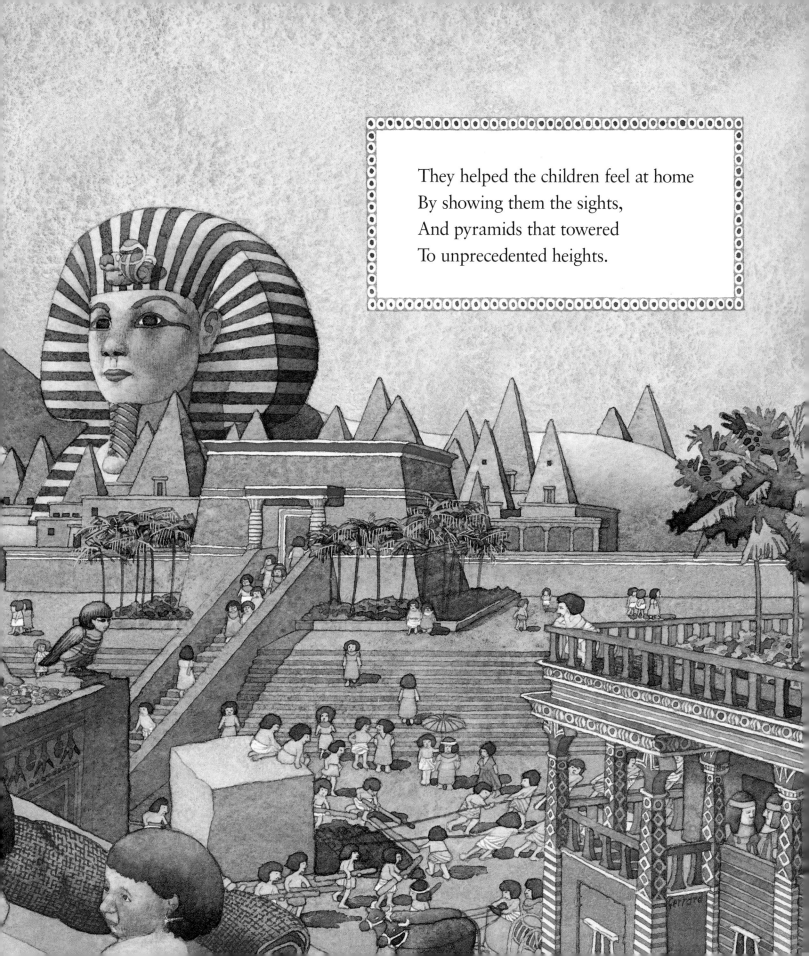

They helped the children feel at home
By showing them the sights,
And pyramids that towered
To unprecedented heights.

Their guardian, who sculpted stone,
Taught Hamut with a will.
He learned to fashion statues
With the most astounding skill.

Gerrard

And pretty soon, when Nekatu
Found she could paint and draw,
Egyptians stood around her
To admire and gasp in awe.

The sculptor, keen to demonstrate
The work these youngsters did,
Proposed that they should help him
With the latest pyramid.
Deep in subterranean chambers
Where sunlight never falls,
They carved and painted wonders
Over all the passage walls.

The King came by to see the work
And almost had a fit—
In all his royal life he'd
Never seen the likes of it!
He asked them both to fabricate
His dear Queen's birthday treat,
A piece so rare and special
It would make her day complete.

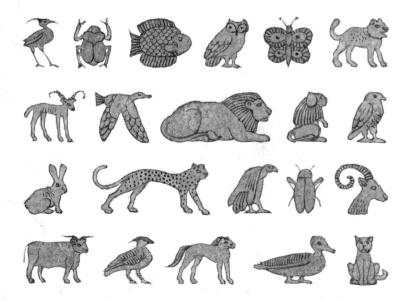

The children, who were thrilled to be
Commissioned by the King,
Began at once to fashion
An exquisite sort of thing.

And when at last their work was done,
They had a bath and dressed,
And went to join the party
At the palace, with the rest.

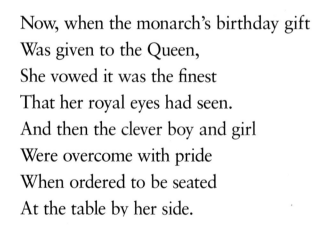

Now, when the monarch's birthday gift
Was given to the Queen,
She vowed it was the finest
That her royal eyes had seen.
And then the clever boy and girl
Were overcome with pride
When ordered to be seated
At the table by her side.

Then these two junior geniuses
Achieved enormous fame,
While managing to stay both
Shy and modest, just the same.
But Fate held quite a shock in store,
Because, it's sad to say,
Some canny villains kidnapped
Them, and carried them away!

These ruffians knew very well
That kings in foreign parts
Paid handsomely for slaves so
Deft and skillful in the arts.
And though the children struggled hard,
Their efforts came to naught;
The twosome were held captive
On a boat that left the port.

But once again Fate intervened,
Because the floods arrived
And sank the scoundrels' vessel.
But the lucky pair survived,
Thanks to their pal the crocodile,
Who'd always stayed around—
He braved the floods and thereby
Saved his friends from being drowned.

They clung like limpets to his sides
Until the floods had passed.
Then on his back they clambered
For the journey home at last.
So, pausing just to thank their friends,
They traveled home in style,
Though not by boat or chariot,
But by first-class crocodile.

Then brave Hamut and Nekatu
Came home to scenes of joy,
And there were hugs and kisses
For the long-lost girl and boy.
And at the celebration feast
The children praised their friend,
The constant crocodile who
Gave this tale a happy end.

Library of Congress catalog card number: 93-74143
First published in Great Britain by Victor Gollancz, 1994
Printed in Belgium by Proost
First American edition, 1994

To learn more about hieroglyphics, the author would like
to suggest Catharine Roehrig's *Fun with Hieroglyphs*.